KU-033-145

For Ems, Mum and Dad and for Adèle

LITTLE TIGER PRESS
An imprint of Magi Publications
1 The Coda Centre, 189 Munster Road,
London SW6 6AW
www.littletigerpress.com
First published in Great Britain 2004
This edition published 2008
Text and illustrations copyright © Rory Tyger 2004
Rory Tyger has asserted their rights to be identified
as the author and illustrator of this work under
the Copyright, Designs and Patents Act, 1988
All rights reserved
ISBN 978 1 84506 813 4
A CIP catalogue record for this book is available
from the British Library
Printed in China
2 4 6 8 10 9 7 5 3 1

newton
and the big mess

by Rory Tyger

LITTLE TIGER PRESS
London

PITTER PATTER! PLIP PLOP!

It was raining.

"Look, Snappy!" said Newton. "Lots of big puddles to jump in. What fun! Let's go splish-splashing. I'll get my coat and wellies and then we'll be ready."

Newton found his raincoat
and umbrella hanging by the door.
Then he found . . .

. . . one wellington.

"That's strange, Snappy," he said.
"I'm sure I was wearing both boots
last time I went splashing!
Wherever can the
other one be?"

Newton looked
for his wellington
all over the house.
He looked in the toybox.

He looked under the bed.
He even looked in the bed!
But he couldn't find it anywhere!

"I know!" said Newton.
"It must be in the cupboard
under the stairs."

Newton pulled open the cupboard
door a little bit and peered inside.
It was very dark. He saw a huge
jumble of shapes.

"Don't be scared, Snappy,"
he said. "I'll turn on the light."

Newton opened
the door and gasped.
"Oh my!" he said.
"Come on, Snappy,
I'm going to need
your help!"

Newton waded into the clutter and started searching for his missing wellie boot.

Newton searched
deeper and deeper
in the cupboard,
flinging things over
his shoulder as
he went.

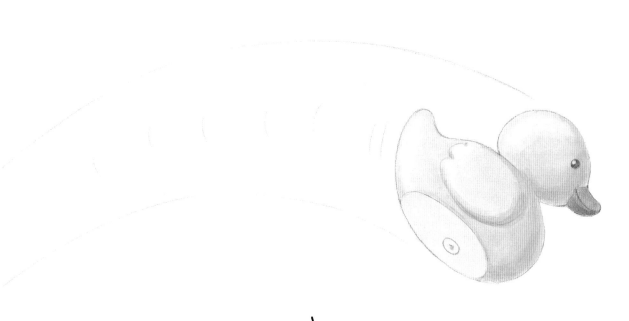

"Bat!" WHEE! BONK!

"Ooooh! Pong! A smelly sock!" WHEE! SPLAT!
"Sorry, Snappy!"

"Rubber duck!" WHEE! BOING! BOUNCE!

Newton stopped and held up a shiny
red rain hat.

"I thought I'd lost that!" he said.

At last, in the deepest, darkest part of the cupboard, Newton found the missing wellington.

"Hooray! I knew it was here," he cried.

"Now, let's go quickly before the rain stops and the puddles go away!"

Newton pulled on his wellington and looked at his shiny red feet.

Then he looked around him. "What a mess we've made, Snappy!" he said. "But there's no time to tidy up now. We can do it later."

Newton threw everything
back into the cupboard as
quickly as he could.
He leaned against the door
and, with a huge heave,
he shut it.
  "Right then, Snappy.
Let's go splashing!"
Newton cried.

"Snappy? . . .

 . . . Snappy?"

Newton looked around, but he guessed
where Snappy must be – he'd stuffed
him into the cupboard
by mistake!

Newton looked anxiously at the door.
There was only one thing to do.

"Don't worry, Snappy. I'm coming
to rescue you."

Newton took a deep breath and
turned the door handle as
gently as he could . . .

WHAM!
BANG!
CRASH!

Everything came tumbling
out of the cupboard, covering
Newton like a huge wave.
"Yikes!" said Newton.
"I thought that might
happen!"

As Newton scrambled to his feet he saw
just what he needed. It was a shiny helmet.

"Emergency! Newton to the rescue!" he called.
And he set to work, clearing the cupboard.

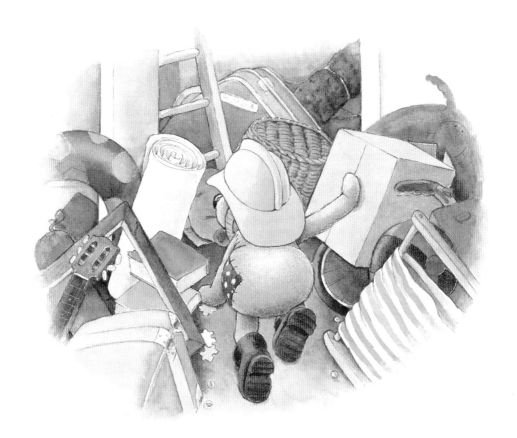

CRASH! BANG! CLATTER! CLUNK!

Soon there were only a few things left in the cupboard and Newton was getting worried.
He was sure that Snappy was lost forever.

Newton picked up an old coat and was about to throw it away when he spotted something.

"Snappy? Is that you?" he said. Newton looked closer and sure enough, there was Snappy.

"Hooray!"

Newton gave Snappy the biggest hug. "Poor Snappy," he said. "And all because of this big, big mess. I don't EVER want to lose you again."

Then something amazing happened. Newton started to put things away, and he didn't stop until everything was tidy and in its proper place. "Now, Snappy," he said,

"let's go splashing!"

And so they did!